Too-Small Tyson

JaNay Brown-Wood

Illustrated by
Anastasia Magloire Williams

Charlesbridge

Tyson has four brothers: Thomas, Thaddeus, Tyrell, and Terrance. Tyson is the youngest. And the smallest.

When they play basketball, Tyson always seems to run
around more than anybody else.

"I have to take way more steps to go as far as you guys,"
Tyson tells his brothers.

"Well, Li'l Man," says Terrance, "your steps are smaller."

Yep, Tyson is definitely the little man of the family.

But Tyson is bigger than some things, like Swish, who is the family's pet gerbil and Tyson's best friend.

Swish loves climbing through the tubes in his cage and eating snacks right out of Tyson's hand. Apples are Swish's favorite.

After the game it's time to clean Swish's cage.
"I can help!" Tyson calls.

"Don't worry about it, Li'l Man," Tyrell says. "We got it."
Tyson's brothers never let him help.

But when they go inside, Swish's cage is empty!

"Don't worry about it, Li'l Man," Thomas says. "We'll take care of it."

Tyson wishes he could search with his brothers. Instead, he finds his own way to help.

Tyson grabs the tubes from Swish's cage and heads for the kitchen. He begins washing the tubes so they'll be nice and clean when his brothers bring Swish back.

There are short tubes, medium tubes, and long tubes.

Tyson joins the search. He thinks about what it'd be like to be as small-small-small as Swish.

"If I were Swish, where would I go?" Tyson crawls on his hands and knees, pretending to be a gerbil.

"There he is!" shouts Tyson. "I'll get him!"

Swish is hiding under the far corner of the bed, but Tyson's arm is too short to reach.

"Don't worry about it, Li'l Man. We got it," Thaddeus says. But Swish scurries just out of reach.

Thomas, Tyrell, and Terrence all try. None of them can get to Swish.

How are we gonna get Swish out?

What if . . .

Tyson races to the kitchen and returns with Swish's tubes.

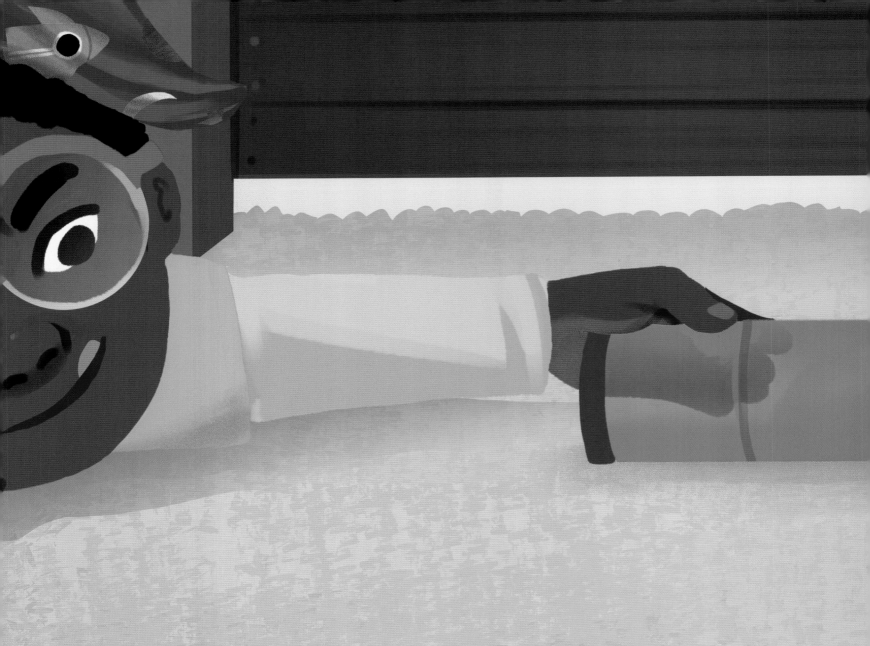

He grabs one long tube. "Now I can reach a lot farther!" he says.

But when he stretches out his arm with the long tube in hand, he still can't reach Swish.

"Good try, Li'l Man," Tyrell says. "Swish will come out when he's ready. Let's go play some more ball."

"Don't worry, Swish," says Tyson. "I'm not leaving you. Maybe . . ."

He grabs a second long tube. Two long tubes might reach all the way to Swish.

But when Tyson accidentally bumps the bed, one long tube rolls off and under it!

Tyson looks around for another long tube. But Swish's cage only had two.

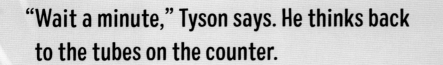

"Wait a minute," Tyson says. He thinks back to the tubes on the counter.

"I need three mediums!"

"One medium, two mediums . . . Aw man!
Where is that other medium, Swish?"

SQUEAK!

"I won't give up, Swish," Tyson says.
"I'm gonna find a way to get you."

I'll use two
short tubes instead!

Tyson grabs the two short tubes and snaps all the tubes together.

"Look!" he says to Swish. "All of these are the same as *two* long tubes!"

Tyson slides the connected tubes under the bed. He reaches Swish!

But the gerbil won't budge. And Tyson's brothers are back to see what's up.

Just like that, Swish climbs through the tube, all the way to the apple in Tyson's hand. Tyson cuddles his best friend close.

"Well, how about that!" says Terrance. "Good job, Li'l Man."

Tyson has four brothers. He's the youngest. And the smallest.
But he's just the right size to lend a helping hand.

Author's Note

As an author, I am often inspired to write stories that celebrate Black characters living their lives—just the way I live mine or you live yours. I strive to write books that were not readily available to me when I was a child—books that mirror the experiences of many Black children all across the country. I want readers to see characters that look like them in stories about family relationships, joy, or overcoming obstacles. I want to show Black characters celebrating and playing and doing just about *everything*—including mathematical thinking. That way, readers come to understand that they belong in a wide variety of books and that they, too, are capable of overcoming obstacles.

While many of my characters are Black, it is important for stories to include diverse characters from *all* backgrounds and experiences—so that we discover characters that are similar to *and* different from us. The specific details of who we are make our stories that much more memorable and interesting. We can all be problem solvers, no matter where we come from, what we look like, what pet we have, or how big or small our family may be! Just like Tyson.

—JaNay Brown-Wood

Exploring the Math

Tyson is too small to do some things, but when his beloved gerbil, Swish, gets lost, he is determined to come to the rescue. As Tyson looks for just the right combination of tubes to reach Swish under the bed, he uses proportional thinking. He comes to see that the smaller the tubes, the more tubes he'll need to span the distance.

When children explore proportional relationships like Tyson does, they begin to gain a foundation for concepts important in measurement, fractions, and algebra.

Try This!

- **Invite children to draw** a gerbil play space made of long, medium, and short tubes. Ask them how they decided which size tubes to draw.

- **Encourage substitutions** as children build with blocks of different sizes. For instance, "If you run out of long blocks, what could you use instead?"

- **Have children pretend** to be a gerbil. Ask, "Which of Swish's tubes would you rather run through: a long green one or a short blue one? Why?"

- **Point out proportions.** Find two or three smaller items the same size as a larger one. For example, "Look! Three baby carrots are as long as this big carrot."

As children explore how many same-size small items make up a larger one, they are developing math skills. And, like Tyson, they may find that sometimes being the smallest can be an advantage!

—Folashade Cromwell Solomon, EdD
Associate Professor, Department of Education,
Framingham State University, and Research Scientist, TERC

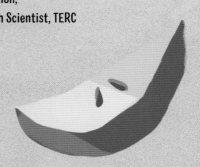

Visit **www.charlesbridge.com/storytellingmath** for more activities.

To Dr. Mariama Smith Gray and your beautiful and inspiring family.—J. B-W.

For all of the "too-smalls" out there, like Tyson and me: Keep thinking smart and embrace your creativity!—A. M. W.

This book is supported in part by TERC under a grant from the Heising-Simons Foundation.

At the time of publication, all URLs printed in this book were accurate and active. Charlesbridge, TERC, the author, and the illustrator are not responsible for the content or accessibility of any website.

Developed in conjunction with TERC
2067 Massachusetts Avenue
Cambridge, MA 02140
(617) 873-9600
www.terc.edu

Published by Charlesbridge
9 Galen Street
Watertown, MA 02472
(617) 926-0329
www.charlesbridge.com

Printed in China
(hc) 10 9 8 7 6 5 4 3 2 1
(pb) 10 9 8 7 6 5 4 3

Library of Congress Cataloging-in-Publication Data
Names: Brown-Wood, JaNay, author. | Williams, Anastasia Magloire, illustrator.
Title: Too-small Tyson / JaNay Brown-Wood, illustrations by Anastasia Magloire Williams.
Description: Watertown, MA: Charlesbridge Publishing, [2022] | Series: [Storytelling math] | Audience: Ages 3–6. | Audience: Grades K–1. | Summary: As the smallest of five brothers, Tyson is used to being left out, but when the family's pet gerbil, Swish, escapes, it is Tyson's creative thinking and mathematical skills that save the day.
Identifiers: LCCN 2020026149 (print) | LCCN 2020026150 (ebook) | ISBN 9781623541644 (hardcover) | ISBN 9781623542009 (trade paperback) | ISBN 9781632899514 (ebook)
Subjects: CYAC: Size—Fiction. | Proportion—Fiction. | Creative thinking—Fiction. | Brothers—Fiction. | African Americans—Fiction. | Gerbils—Fiction.
Classification: LCC PZ7.B81983 Too 2022 (print) | LCC PZ7.B81983 (ebook) | DDC [E]—dc23
LC record available at https://lccn.loc.gov/2020026149
LC ebook record available at https://lccn.loc.gov/2020026150

Illustrations done in digital media
Display type set in Kora Kora by HansCo Studios
Text type set in Colby Condensed by Jason Vandenberg
Printed by 1010 Printing International
    Limited in Huizhou, Guangdong, China
Production supervision by Jennifer Most Delaney
Designed by Jon Simeon